SUSAN G.

Illustrated by Jess Mikhail

OXFORD
UNIVERSITY PRESS

OXFORD
UNIVERSITY PRESS

Great Clarendon Street, Oxford OX2 6DP

Oxford University Press is a department of the University of Oxford.
It furthers the University's objective of excellence in research, scholarship,
and education by publishing worldwide in

Oxford New York
Auckland Cape Town Dar es Salaam Hong Kong Karachi
Kuala Lumpur Madrid Melbourne Mexico City Nairobi
New Delhi Shanghai Taipei Toronto

With offices in
Argentina Austria Brazil Chile Czech Republic France Greece
Guatemala Hungary Italy Japan Poland Portugal Singapore
South Korea Switzerland Thailand Turkey Ukraine Vietnam

Oxford is a registered trade mark of Oxford University Press
in the UK and in certain other countries

British Library Cataloguing in Publication Data
Data available

ISBN 978-0-19-91349-1

3 5 7 9 10 8 6 4 2

Available in packs
Stage 10 More Stories B Pack of 6:
ISBN 978-0-19-911343-9
Stage 10 More Stories B Class Pack:
ISBN 978-0-19-911344-6
Guided Reading Cards also available:
ISBN 978-0-19-911352-1

Printed in China by Imago

1

Micro arrives

On Daniel's birthday, he woke up and found a big box by his bed. It looked like a kennel.

'A dog!' cried Daniel. He'd wanted a dog for ages.

He leapt out of bed and opened the kennel door.

There was Micro. He was shiny and silver, with yellow flashing eyes.

'That isn't a real dog,' said Daniel.

'I know,' said Mum. 'But real dogs aren't allowed in our flats. Just look what Micro can do.'

Mum turned to Micro. 'Walk,' she said.

Micro stumped across the carpet on stiff, jerky legs.

'Bark,' said Mum.

Micro opened his metal mouth. Was he barking? It was hard to tell. It was such a soft little sound. 'Yip, yip, yip, yip, yip.'

'Wag your tail,' said Mum.

Micro's metal tail made a whirring sound as it went one way, then the other.

'But I wanted a *real* dog,' said Daniel. He was deeply disappointed.

'Micro's *better* than a real dog,' said Mum. 'He's not noisy or messy. He always does what he's told. Go on. Tell him to do something.'

'Go back in your kennel, Micro,' said Daniel.

Micro turned round and clunked back into his box.

'What a good dog!' said Mum to Micro. 'I think you're the perfect pet.'

But Daniel didn't seem to think so. He said, 'Thanks, Mum.' Then he ripped open the rest of his presents.

All day and all night, Micro waited.

But Daniel played with his other presents. He didn't take Micro out once.

Slowy, inside his dark box, Micro's eyes lost their brightness.

2

Micro starts thinking

Next morning, as Daniel left for school, Mum called after him, 'You're late, Daniel. WALK FAST!'

Alone in his dark box, Micro heard, 'WALK FAST'.

His robot brain started whirring. His little yellow eyes lit up as bright as ever.

He came trundling out of his kennel.

He raced along on his stumpy legs, across the carpet. He went out through the open glass doors and he only stopped when his red nose hit the balcony.

'CLANG!'

Daniel's mum didn't see him. She was too busy getting ready for work.

Micro looked down from the seventh floor. He could see the park, with green trees and grass. He saw people and furry things with four legs running about.

Suddenly, Micro's brain started thinking for itself.

'Those are *real* dogs,' thought Micro.

He saw the real dogs running after sticks and balls.

'Those real dogs are playing,' thought Micro.

They weren't shut up and left alone by their owners in dark boxes.

His bright eyes glowed like fire. His robot brain whirred again. With every thought, it got more and more clever. Now it was making plans.

‘I will go down there,’ decided Micro, ‘and I’ll watch the real dogs. I will learn how to be like them. Then Daniel will play with me.’

But how could he get to the park? He was high up and the park was a long way down.

3

What real dogs do

Micro went back and hid behind the sofa. Then he saw his chance.

Daniel's mum went to work and Micro sneaked out through the door after her.

He saw her press a button in the wall. Then she vanished through some sliding doors. His robot eyes flashed.

'That is the way down,' he decided.

He got up on his back legs. With his metal nose, he pressed the same button.

DING! The lift came. Micro walked in. He rode down to the ground floor. The people in the lift with him stared. They looked puzzled, but no one said anything.

In the park, Micro peeked out from behind a tree. He saw the dog owners shout, ‘Come here!’ The real dogs took no notice. They ran off.

He saw the dog owners shout, ‘Be quiet!’

But the real dogs barked even louder: ‘RUFF! RUFF! RUFF!’

The dogs didn't do what they were told to do. But their owners still seemed to love them. They patted their heads and scratched them behind the ears.

Micro thought, 'If I do what real dogs do, Daniel might scratch behind *my* ears.'

Micro knew he still had a lot to learn. So he followed a dog called Scruffy.

Scruffy ran into his house like a mad thing, chasing his own tail.

Micro stood on his back legs and peeked through an open window. Scruffy chewed the carpet. He drank from the toilet bowl.

Then a little girl came in and put her arms round Scruffy's neck and hugged him.

'You're the best dog in the world,' she said.

'*I* want to be the best dog in the world,' thought Micro, and now he knew how to do it.

4
'What's the matter with you?'

Micro went back home. He rode up to the seventh floor in the lift. Daniel's mum came back from work and he sneaked into the flat behind her.

'Why are you out of your box?' said Daniel's mum, surprised. 'Get back into your kennel.'

But Micro ran the other way.

He opened his metal mouth. 'Ruff! Ruff! Ruff!' he roared, as he'd heard the real dogs do.

Daniel's mum covered her ears, 'Shhh! What a racket!'

Micro barked even louder, 'RUFF! RUFF! RUFF!' He rushed round in a circle, chasing his tail, until he was just a silver blur.

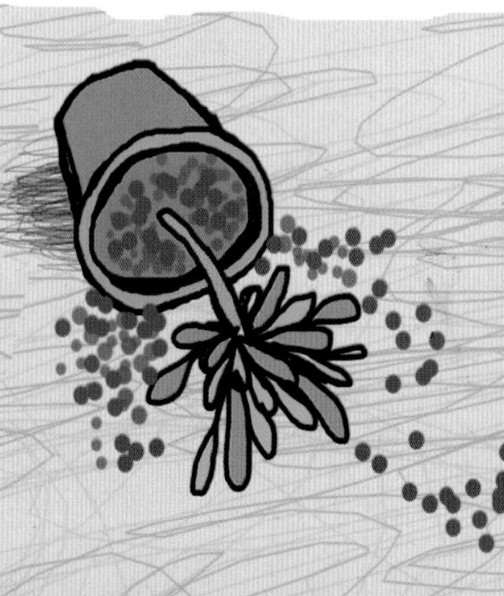

He jumped up at Daniel's mum.

'Get down!' she said.

But Micro took no notice and jumped up even more.

With his metal jaws, he chomped great bits out of the carpet.

'Stop that, now!' yelled Daniel's mum. 'What's the matter with you? You're supposed to be a good dog!'

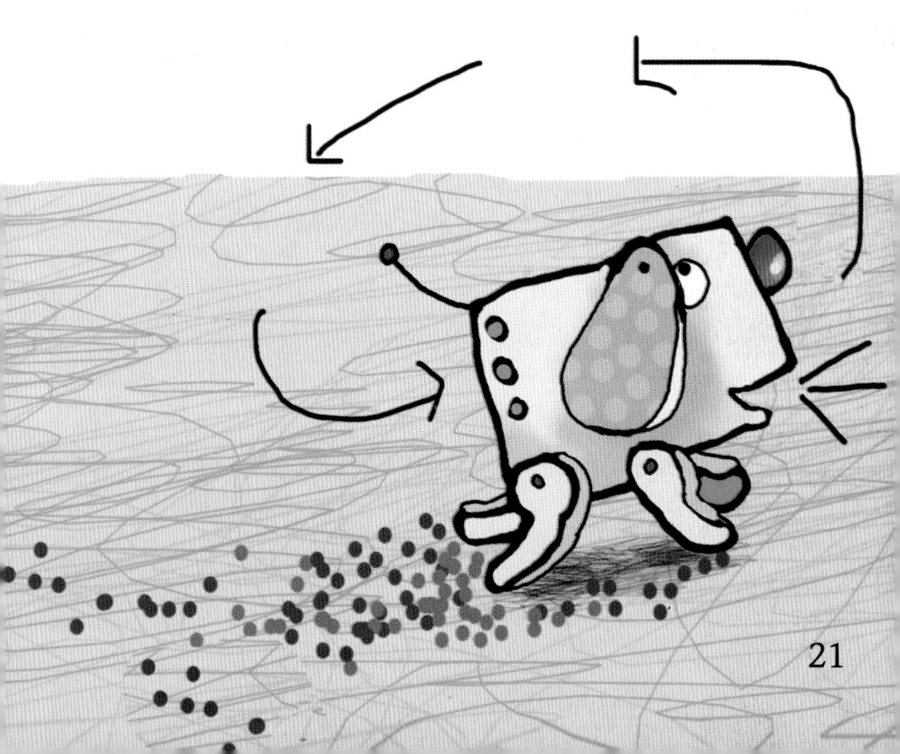

Micro rushed into the bathroom. He stuck his head down the toilet, just as he'd seen Scruffy do.

Then he pulled his head out and shook water all over the place.

It was the last straw. 'I'm not putting up with this!' said Daniel's mum. 'The stupid machine has gone mad!'

She grabbed Micro. She took him out of the flat and threw him down the rubbish chute.

'Daniel never played with it anyway,' she thought. 'He won't even miss it.'

Dented and battered, Micro lay in the dark basement with the rubbish bags.

'What did I do wrong?' he thought sadly. 'I was only doing what real dogs do.'

But, instead of being loved, he'd been thrown out with the rubbish.

5

Where is Micro?

Mum was right. When Daniel came home from school, he didn't even notice that Micro was missing.

But he did notice the chewed carpet.

'Who did that?' he said.

Mum said, 'That dog! When I came home it went crazy! It was barking and chasing around in circles. It even stuck its head down the toilet.'

Mum went on, 'I said, "Stop it!" but it took no notice! Just as if it had a mind of its own!'

'Really?' said Daniel. 'A mind of its own?'

For the first time, he was interested in Micro. He said, 'Where is he?'

Mum looked a bit uncomfortable. 'I threw him down the rubbish chute,' she said.

'What!' yelled Daniel. 'You threw my dog down the rubbish chute! How could you? He was my birthday present!'

Daniel rushed for the door.

'Where are you going?' said Mum.

'To the basement. To find Micro!'

Mum felt really bad now. She called out after Daniel, 'I didn't think you wanted him!'

In the basement, Daniel saw a glint of silver among the rubbish bags.

'Micro!' he cried.

Micro's eyes lit up. He jumped up and tried to lick Daniel's face with his metal tongue.

Daniel picked him up in his arms and carried him outside. 'Stay here,' he said to Micro.

But Micro was already racing towards the park. He'd seen Scruffy!

With joyful barks, Micro ran to Scruffy on his stumpy, metal legs. His tail was wagging, even though no one had told it to.

Daniel watched, amazed. Micro and Scruffy raced around together. They dug holes. They chased seagulls. They were having the time of their lives.

Daniel threw a stick. 'Fetch, Micro!' he cried.

Of course, Micro ran the other way.

He fetched back an empty pizza box, and dropped it at Daniel's feet.

Daniel grinned, 'You silly dog.'

Then Daniel patted Micro's head. He scratched him behind his shiny, silver ears.

'I always wanted a dog,' he said. 'and now I've got one.'

He put his arms around Micro's metal neck. 'I've got the best dog in the world.'

About the author

How did I get the idea for Micro the Metal Dog? I read an article in a magazine. It said that, when old people go into care homes, they often can't take their pet dogs with them. That makes them very unhappy. So, in Japan, they're planning to offer people robot pet dogs instead.

I thought, 'How can a robot pet dog ever be as good as the real thing?'
Well, it can't. Unless, of course, it's Micro the Metal Dog!